H*E FOR THE HOLIDAY

T. ASHLEY

Copyright © 2020 by T. Ashley

All rights reserved.

No part of this book may be reproduced in any form or by any electronic or mechanical means, including information storage and retrieval systems, without written permission from the author, except for the use of brief quotations in a book review.

*This book isn't dedicated to anyone because it is waaaaay too raunchy.
Well, it's dedicated to the lovers of raunch.*

PART I
THE SET UP

1

NOVA

The tarmac was covered in snow, and all I could think of was how thankful I was that my plane had landed safely. I made a mental note to give a hefty Christmas bonus to my flight crew for getting me here in such a horrendous storm and in good time. It was a last-minute trip home to New York from Tennessee where I owned a lucrative management company. I really didn't take many days off from running my business, but my mother insisted that I take some time off to see her. After receiving too many text messages, phone calls, and emails, I finally caved. So, here I am. Cold, aggravated, and feeling like I left too much work behind for all of this white shit all over the ground.

I could see a black Sedan idling near the entrance of the small airport – if you would call it that. I waited, hugging my body, trying to conjure any source of cold, praying that the driver would see me and come save me from the treacherous cold. The car did not move, so I made my way towards it, praying that I wouldn't face plant onto the pavement.

When I finally made it to the car, a tall man stepped out of the driver's side and pulled open the back door. I wasn't going to let him think that this behavior was okay, so I didn't bother to make an eye contact or thank him for his gesture. It was his job to open doors for his clients, the fuck I look like thanking him while the wetness was seeping through to my socks? He grunted before the door shut behind me, and I swear I almost heard him curse under his breath.

We rode in silence as the car zipped out of the airport. He was driving a little too reckless for me, so I sent a quick text to my assistant.

Me: Next time, make sure the driver is in a weather appropriate car.

Shelly: The Sprint subscriber is temporarily out of service.

Me: I literally watched the bubbles on my screen as you typed that.

Shelly: He was the only one available at short notice. I'm sorry.

Me: Enjoy your time off. I will try and keep the texts to a minimum.

Shelly: Just sent an email over to the owner asking if he has a better vehicle to carry my princess boss in.

Just as I was reading the text, the driver's phone pinged, and he looked down to read

whatever just came through.

Me: Also, let him know that his driver is texting and driving.

Shelly: Done.

His phone pinged again, and he continued to look at it. It wasn't until I saw his chocolate eyes staring at me with such hatred that I realized that he was probably the owner receiving complaints from my assistant.

"Shit," I whispered and slid lower into my seat. It was about a two-hour ride, and the tension in the air just went from a four to a ten in a matter of seconds. Needless to say, this was going to be a long ride. I longed to take off my shoes and spread out to the row across from me, but I was sure I was too short. Even if I could reach, I wouldn't catch myself dead doing such a thing.

The driver cleared his throat, "Ma'am, I'm sorry the conditions of the car are not up to your standards." I watched his eyes snapping back and forth from me to the road. "We have an entire fleet of suitable vehicles, but this was very last minute, and I couldn't prepare properly. Your assistant insisted that I get to the airport as soon as possible; this was the only car available. Please accept my sincerest apology, and I ensure you that it will be replaced."

Did he just wink at me? I questioned, and unfortunately, that dark side of me responded. *Yes, bitch, he just winked at you! You know you love a nice piece of chocolate with dimples accenting his smile.*

He was fine. Well, from what I could see at this angle. Dark. Chocolate. Tall. Smelled good. Owned his own company. Check. Check. Triple check. I tried to get a better look at his entire physique, however, I couldn't quite see it all through the mirror, so I just sat back and pouted. The car was nice, but parts of me wanted to just complain about anything.

"Everything okay back there?"

"Huh? What?" I snapped up straight. I needed to get myself together.

He chuckled. It was deep and throaty, and my mind quickly snapped to what it would sound like moaning in my ear.

Bitch! I thought. *Get it together.*

"Well, I just apologized, and you turned from ice queen to sad puppy princess – usually apologies put people in better moods, not worse."

"Oh, I was just thinking about how long I would have to spend in this awful car." I internally slapped myself, I seriously didn't need to be this rude to the guy who was clearly just moving in action for my impatient ass. "I'm sorry, what is your name?"

He turned his head towards me, giving me a full view of that plump and dimpled cheek, licked his lips, and said, "Chaz."

"Oh."

"Oh?"

"Oh."

"Oh, okay." He turned his focus back to the road. "So, Miss Nova, what brings you to the good state of New York all the way from Tennessee?"

"Hold up. How did you know all of that?"

"So, we have this little thing called a contract, and your assistant sent over your flight itinerary." He held up a clipboard. "You sure everything's okay? You seem a little -"

I cut him off. "A little what? Just because I am a black woman with money, people always assumin' that I have a stuck-up personality or am a bitch. I'm just trying to live my life without all of the other bullshit."

Chaz went silent. Like scary silent. Like, *I need to text someone and let them know where I am* silent. I watched him as he looked at me in the rearview mirror then back to the road. I must have said something very wrong to make him grow so quiet.

I cleared my throat, "Did I say something wrong?"

Before he could answer, my inner annoying bitch chimed in. *Bitch! You just went postal on the dude, and he didn't do anything wrong!*

Chaz looked at me in the mirror. "Nah, I was just going to say that you seem a little stressed out. All of that proved that my speculation wasn't wrong." He moved a little in the front seat, but kept talking, "I mean this in the most..." —he thought about the words carefully— "respectful client-customer manner. That type of mouth? A mouth like yours? It could use a little discipline."

I laughed. "What? Like washing it out with soap?"

"No. Not like that." He gave a full-on panty-dropping smile that made my thighs clench together.

My nerves were rising from the pit of my stomach to the back of my throat, but I wasn't going to back down. "Like throw me over your lap and spank me into discipline?"

"That's a little closer to what I was thinking." He winked again.

"' A little closer'? Well, you're going to have to be a little more specific." I put on my best sexy voice as I spoke to him. "Because I could use some discipline."

"Is that so, Miss Nova?"

"It is."

"Sir."

"Sir?"

His eyes shot up to the rearview mirror. "Yes, Nova."

"I am so confused right now."

"Don't be." I swear his eyes darkened a shade or two, and his voice deepened. "When you address me, it will be as 'Sir'. Do you understand?"

I sat silently, contemplating how I was going to respond, and the only thing I could do is laugh. I laughed so hard, it felt like a weight was lifted off of my chest. I guess I needed a good laugh. When I finally got myself together and wiped the tears from my eyes, the car was no longer moving, and Chaz was exiting his door. The front door slammed, and the door to the back swung open.

Chaz climbed into the backseat with me with this strange smirk on his face. "Do you understand?"

"Oh, so you're for real?"

He leaned in closer to me and ran the pad of his thumb down my jawline. "I don't know why you think I'm playing around."

I looked out of the window, granted they were tinted, but I wasn't about to just let it all hang out there on the side of the interstate. The snow had picked up heavily, and I think I was more worried about making it safely to my mother's place.

Chaz moved my chin to face him. "They can't see you. I promise."

"I'm sure you say that to all the females silly enough to partake in your backseat escapades."

"I take pride in being respectful when it comes to my business." He sat with his back against the door, and I got a better look at him from this angle. I was positive his body was well taken care of underneath his royal blue sweater and khaki pants--the fabric complimented every muscle.

"What changed?"

He licked his lips. "A fine, little, and disobedient minx decided at the last minute that she wanted to take a ride in the backseat of my car." Chaz raised his eyebrow as if to challenge me—goading me to say otherwise. I just sat there and watched him. He was here, sitting next to me, waiting for my next move.

So, I made it. "Sir, I don't think it is appropriate for me to ask for that spanking your itchy palm desperately wants to give. I don't think a disobedient minx like me should be the one to initiate anything. It is all up to you."

That was all he needed to jump into action. Chaz slid his hand behind my neck, massaged it a little bit, and guided my body closer to his. In my ear, he whispered, "Trust me, follow my lead and relax."

"How can I do that with someone I just met?"

"Once I get started, you won't have to worry about all of that." Grabbing a handful of my curls, he gave a small yank making my head tilt backwards and my mouth falling open to gasp. Chaz ran his nose from my jawline to my chin, moving his body to hover over me. Stopping abruptly, he sat down opposite me, pointed at my coat, and waited as I fulfilled his request.

A chill ran down my body as the cool air made contact with my bare arms. Chaz reached up and adjusted the heat in the rear of the car. I gave in and let a smile touch my nervous lips. Chaz saw this and smiled. "Your comfort will always be my number one priority. This won't be fun without it."

Always. What the hell did he mean by "always", and why the hell was I this nervous? I had plenty of experiences—some that would probably put the current one to shame, so why was I feeling so damn out of sorts right now?

Girl, because he looks like he got some good dick and is about to give it to you. Sometimes, my inner thoughts didn't know when it was a good time to show up. Now wasn't the time because I wanted to burst out in laughter from the combination of my brain and my nerves. The better part of my thoughts chimed in, *Just calm down. You got this.*

Yes, I do have this. I'm a successful businesswoman, and it was time that I started acting with some kind of sense. I straightened my back and folded my arms across my chest. *Perfect.* I could feel myself trying to fight an eye roll. Now, I was sitting here looking like a petulant child when all I wanted was to gain some power back in the situation.

"Is there a problem, Miss Nova?" Chaz didn't seem like he cared about an answer, he was just waiting for me to take off my coat. Before I could move, he reached down and pulled my boot covered foot into his lap, causing me to scoot down in the seat. His eyes never left mine as he removed my boot. I sent a silent prayer that in my rush to leave, I had picked a nice pair of socks and not something that I had in my drawer for ages and were worn from often use. My eyes shot down to my foot, and I almost sighed with relief when I realized that I had on a nice pair of socks. I replayed my morning to make sure the same thing for my underwear, and I was pretty sure that I was safe in that department.

My foot jerked forward again, and that is when all my hopes and dreams were answered in one touch. Okay, maybe I was being dramatic, but you would be very happy by what my foot was pressed up against. His penis wasn't even fully hard yet, and I was very impressed. As soon as I tried to get a better feel and maybe harden him a bit more, he pulled my foot away and placed it on top of his thigh. Chaz's eyes dropped down to my blouse and back up to my eyes.

Knowingly, I lifted the shirt up and over my head revealing a lacy black bra that did wonders for my cleavage. His eyes left mine as he lifted my other boot to remove it. I wanted him now. When I went to move forward to try and straddle him, he pushed me back onto the seat and pointed at my jeans. I removed them quicker than I removed any other piece of clothing; as amusement tickled his expression and he began to unzip his pants.

Chaz was a work of chocolate art sitting in front of me. Even fully clothed, I could tell that his body was a gift from God that I wanted to unwrap over and over again.

Once my pants were disposed off on the floor of the car, Chaz tilted his head to the side as if to ask me a silent question. I couldn't figure out what he wanted, so I asked, "What?"

His expression darkened, he leaned forward, grabbed my wrist, and yanked me from my seat. I was in a weird position, but he guided me so that my stomach was pressed against his hardness, and my ass was in the air. I could tell that my pussy was getting wetter every time he made me do something in silence. Before I could think of how much I just wanted him to fuck me, his hand landed with great force across my ass. It stung. It hurt. It felt exhilarating. I was being handled in a way that I never had been handled before, and I was enjoying it immensely. I was usually the one with all the power in all aspects of my life. Men tended to handle me with delicate hands. Maybe they thought I would break. Maybe they thought I would break them. Who knows? All I know is right now, I was not in control, and I liked it.

Chaz's hand met my skin once again. This time lower. It was as if he was trying to pop my pussy. Literally. His hand stayed where it was as he pulled my panties to the side and dipped a finger between my folds. I turned to him just in time to see him sucking my juices from his finger. Goodness, he was sexy. I wanted more, but we were moving at his pace, so I had to just wait. Not for long, I hoped.

2

CHAZ

I REGRETTED AGREEING to all of this the moment I saw her step off her private jet. She was sharp. Milk chocolate skin. Shoulder length curls. Minimal makeup. I doubted she would even entertain me because she seemed to be about her business. Her entire disposition screamed serious brick wall up. She was going to be one tough cookie to crack, but I was always ready for a challenge.

I had done a little research on her before I picked her up. She had a successful management company worth millions. Yeah, I was going to have to turn up the charm. I was instructed to give her the shittiest service but still, treat her respectfully. She apparently got off on being able to complain but also enjoyed walking over people. Honestly, after interacting with her, she just seemed like an overworked female trying to get ahead in the world. She was pretty much the female version of me. Started from nothing and achieved her dreams by age forty.

She was situated across my lap with my penis straining to be pressed up against something other than her stomach. I wanted to bend her over and fuck her, but I was instructed to get as much on her as I could. Slow and steady wins the race. I shouldn't have tasted her because her nectar was everything that I needed right now. Her body was curvy. She was thick in all the right places, and I wanted to just lay my head on her and enjoy her warmth. Focusing on the task at hand, I pushed her off me and pointed to the seat across from me. Nova looked aroused and confused at the same time. When she found her seat, she winced a bit bringing a smile to my face. She had no idea how easy I was taking it on her.

I pointed to her underwear. "Take them off and pleasure yourself."

Nova's head tilted back, and I took a moment to think about my life. I was thirty-eight and at the peak of my success. I wasn't missing much out of life, but I guess I could strive for better. I lived a lifestyle of a Dom for a few years now, so I knew, with her, I had to just get to the point. She would talk herself out of this quicker than I talked her out of her clothes. I have had a lot of experience with her type. Women needing to be controlled a little in their lives because they controlled every other aspect of their lives, or women who intimidated men, so they needed to feel that power taken from them. It was all mutual. Most of them were clients that paid for my services, and some of them were just random encounters.

All of this was going to set me up for life. I would not have to hustle so hard to get clientele for my business since I was promised every account on Nova's roster when they needed transportation. I would be able to sit back and watch my company grow larger than I could ever imagine. I was doing well now, but as I said, I could always do better. Nova was my key to better.

Her moans stopped, and when I looked up at her, confusion was evident on her face. "Well, this is no fun if only one party is playing."

In any other circumstance, this would be fun. Too much fun. However, I wasn't here to play. "Did I tell you to stop?"

"You could join me."

"I could." I pointed back between her legs, never breaking the eye contact, and demanded what I wanted.

My favorite thing to do was to watch a woman please herself. You could learn a lot just by watching. I loved to see someone spread eagle, in all of their glory. I decided to give her inspiration. Pulling out my hard dick, I gave it a few strokes. She was turning me on so much right now, I probably wouldn't last long.

Nova's eyes gave me the indication that she liked what she saw, but this was a game, right? I had to ask, "Like what you see, Miss Nova?"

"Yes, Sir."

I growled at her obedience. "Mmm, good girl." She was close to an orgasm, and I smiled at that. "Did you ask me for my permission to cum, Miss Nova?"

The pace her finger was dipping in and out of her wetness sped up, and when I reached over and slapped her hand, she whimpered. "Did you cum?"

Defiantly, she pushed her shoulders back and said, "Yes."

I yanked her onto my lap again. Her warmth covered my throbbing penis. I slapped her ass five times; each one harder than the one before. By the fourth slap, she was giving me the most satisfying screams I had ever heard. If the situation was different, I would be sure to hear that sound every day. After the fifth slap, I rewarded her with two fingers that she immediately clenched her walls around. My thumb pressed against her tight hole that I hoped I had time to fill later. I wonder if she would let me come up to her room once we got to her hotel. It could get a whole lot nastier with more space.

"I'm going to cum again!" She cried out.

I stopped my assault on her pussy and leaned over to whisper in her ear, "But you didn't ask for permission. Do you want to be punished again?"

She was squirming on my lap, trying to get me to finger her again. The friction it was causing to my dick felt so good, but I wanted to bust while pumping into her wet cunt, not on her stomach as she laid across my lap.

"May I cum, please?"

"You're catching on quickly. But, no." I felt her physically deflate with disappointment. "You may, however, suck my dick."

Nova slid off my lap and licked her lips. All I remember thinking before she started was, *Oh, shit*. Nova knew what the fuck she was doing. With every swirl of her tongue and the little gag reflex she had, I knew I was in trouble. She sucked me like her life depended on it, and I had to fight every part of my being to not cum all over her face when she put my balls in her mouth.

"Holy fuck, Nova. You gotta stop, or else I won't be able to fuck that sweet cunt of yours." I damn near lost my mind when she looked up at me, with my dick in her mouth and shrugged.

I think I shocked us both with how quickly I moved. Pushing her back, she fell against the seat behind her, and I didn't show any remorse. She just went ham on my dick, and I was about to repay her kindness.

"Turn around." I pulled my pants off and gabbed a condom out of my wallet in the center console of the front seat.

Once I was wrapped up safely, I got down on the floor of the car and said a silent prayer of gratitude for this extended back seat. I was a tall motherfucker, but when I was told to bring my shittiest car, I knew this one would have to do. It wasn't my best, but it wasn't my worst. It was just right. I gave her a few light taps on the ass and guided her knees up onto the seat. This would be a better angle for me to get a taste before I fucked the shit out of her.

Her moans vibrated through her entire body as I lapped up her nectar. When she was close to cumming again, I stopped and pulled her back down to me. Sliding in easily, Nova finally spoke real words, "Oh, God."

"Miss Nova, you feel so good. Squeeze my dick with your pussy." She did as she was told over and over again. As I fucked her from behind, I reached around to lubricate my thumb with her juices. I made small circles on her clit, and Nova went wild. "Not yet, Miss Nova."

"Please?" she begged, throwing her ass back, meeting every thrust. "Please?" she said again.

My dick wanted to give in, but it felt too good to end this quickly. I pulled my thumb away, and it seemed to calm her a bit, but what I was going to do next would send us both over the edge. I pressed my thumb to her tight hole that was waiting for me.

"I've never—"

I leaned over and whispered while I slowed my thrust, "Just relax. I got this." She took a deep breath, and I pressed into her hole. Her screams. Her wetness. Her tightness. "You may cum now, Miss Nova."

We both came. My name on her lips. A growl between my teeth. God, I hope she would let me come up for more play.

Sitting back and catching my breath, I watched as reality hit Nova. This was going to go either bad or really fucking bad. However, she shocked the hell out of me when she just smiled at me and began to pull on her clothes. Once I was done dressing and about to step out of the car, she was all business again when she asked, "How far are we from the hotel?"

I don't know why my jaw was on the fucking floor, but excuse me as I pick it up and answer her question, "About five minutes."

We rode those five minutes in silence. There was so much going through my head. At first, I regretted what I was about to do, then I thought about the way she just dismissed me after being so intimate with one another, and I was back on track with the plan. When I pulled up to the hotel, she was already out of the car once I climbed out.

I passed the bellhop her bags and turned to say goodbye to Nova, but she just breezed by me like I was nothing. It was all good because I hit send on the file in my email and drove off.

3

NOVA

I NEEDED TO GROUND MYSELF. Get back to normality. However, all I could think about was Chaz and him giving me the best orgasm I had ever experienced. When he dropped me off, all I wanted to do was to take him up to my room andmake him top the last one. Once up in my penthouse suite, I sent a text to my mother.

Me: I made it safely.
Mom: Wow, were the roads bad?
Me: Why do you say that?
Mom: You got in two hours later than when you were supposed to.

I looked at the clock, and it confirmed what my mother said. I guess I didn't answer quickly because her face popped up on my phone.

"Hello, Nadine." I sighed as I pulled off my boots.

"Don't 'Hello Nadine' me. First, you arrive two hours late after when you said you would, and then, you don't text back when I ask a question." I got my toughness from my mother, and I wasn't ashamed of it one bit.

"Well, Mother, I was just trying to get undressed so I could order room service and relax in this huge tub. I wasn't ignoring you." To emphasize my statement, I walked into the large bathroom and started running the water.

"Don't you sass me, Nova Lee Wilcox. I just worry about my only child. You know you could have stayed here." My mom softened a little. I was also her rainbow baby, as they called it. After several miscarriages and failed IVF attempts, my father miraculously knocked my mother up at the tender age of forty. I was a soft spot in her hard seventy-three-year-old heart. She often joked that I kept her young and that she'd stay even younger should she had some grandbabies. I was in my prime. An actress assigned to my management company just signed up to play the leading lady in a Denzel movie. This was our biggest account in the five years that I have been in business; babies were nowhere in my near future.

"Mama, you know it is not a vacation sitting over there listening to you and Daddy bickering."

My mother laughed into the receiver. "You stay with the same man for damn near fifty years and see if you two don't bicker nonstop." I could hear my father saying something in the background. "Yeah, she's here. She will be over tomorrow — leave my child alone." My father must have said something funny because my mother started cackling into the phone.

"Lord, only you find that man so funny."

"Oh, hush. Don't be jealous. Just get yourself a man that will keep you laughing for damn near fifty years." My father said something else in the background. "Oh, Al, don't you start. I gotta go, Nova, see you tomorrow." She hung up before I could respond.

One thing you have to understand about my parents is that they have a healthy sex life. I would come home from school, and my mother would be moaning and the walls would be banging. It didn't start bothering me until I would have friends over and they would sneak away to get busy. I thought it was normal, but once I saw my friends' reactions, I guess it wasn't so normal, or maybe their parents needed to take some advice from Al and Nadine's marriage handbook. The sex probably kept them young, not me.

I ordered a bottle of Prosecco, wings, and a slice of chocolate cake.

Listen, I like the finer things in life, but the cheap ones get a girl going. Besides, I didn't grow up privileged. My parents kicked, screamed, and refused to move out of the home they raised me in. My father gave me a speech about working hard to buy his home and move to a better side of the hood. He had tears in his eyes, so I backed off and sold the home that I bought for them. My father expressed how proud he was of me, but that I should use my money for myself. Not anyone else. I just wanted to give back to the people that had my back from day one.

Putting my parents out of my brain, I slid into the tub, and the warm water massaged my sore muscles. Chaz popped into my mind, and I was shocked that my clit throbbed with want. Wishing I had brought my wand with me, I looked over my shoulder and noticed that the shower had a detachable showerhead. Shower it is.

Just as I was letting the water out of the tub, I heard a soft knock at the door. I loved this hotel already because the room service was on point. I grabbed a robe and the twenty bucks off the table to tip the guy, but when I opened it, the smile I wore melted from my face, and I almost became putty on the floor.

"Gavin?" What I really should have said was: What the fuck are you doing here? Get your lying, cheating, no good ass out of here! Nope, I had to be all swoony and say his name.

You all know there's that one person that you will be foolish for every once in a while? Well, that was Gavin for me. Gavin was the finest and only white boy in our neighborhood. We grew up together, and he would forever be my weakness. No matter how hard I tried, I just couldn't let go of the thought of us. I wanted to. I prayed to the gods that he no longer would have this hold on me, but I just couldn't let him go.

He licked his lips, and I wanted to be his tongue being dragged across his bottom lip. "What up, Nova? You know you can't come to town and not see me."

"I'm sure your freeloading ass would have been over to my mama's house tomorrow for dinner." I stepped back and let him into my room. "How'd you know I was staying here?"

"Nova, this my city. I know everything." He hung his coat on a hook next to the door. I got a good look at him then. Broad shoulders. Abs for days. Nice waistline. He wore a grey, long-sleeved Henley thermal, jeans, and Timberland boots. Last time I saw him, he was growing out his beard, but today, he was clean-shaven, and his hair was much shorter than I remembered. Gavin was the first boy I fell in love with and the first man to break my heart. He was always up to something, and when he got my ex-best friend pregnant while I was away at college, that was the last straw. She ended up terminating the pregnancy because of personal reasons. However, after that, Gavin and I were a memory and an occasional hookup.

"You look good, Gavin." I pulled my robe closer to my body.

"You sayin' that like I was strung out on drugs or some shit the last time I saw you." He sat down on the couch.

"Well, with that weird lumberjack look you had going on, I was beginning to worry."

Gavin laughed. "Nova, always with the jokes."

I sighed. "What are you doing here, Gavin?"

"I didn't think I needed a reason to see my favorite girl." He patted the seat next to him.

"Gavin."

"Nova."

I sat next to him. "Seriously, was it my mama?"

"Nah, Mama Nadine is like a vault when it comes to you. This my Place."

"What do you mean, this is your place?" It hit me then. He always said he would open a bar or a nightclub or something and call it "Place".

A picture of a twelve-year-old Gavin popped into my mind. Wire weaving through his teeth. Unruly light brown, curly hair. And the brightest green eyes that I used to lose myself in. He used to say to me all of the time, "I'm going to call it 'Place' so people would be like 'I'm going to the Place' and others would be like 'Where?' It's a conversation starter, Nova." It was clever. He was the smartest kid I knew. I know better now. There were definitely smarter out there, but what did my ten-year-old self know?

Shelly raved about this place and told me that I must stay here. I wanted to slap her. One drunken night, I cried to her about Gavin. I let it all out and then made her swear that she wouldn't tell a soul. She had to know that Gavin Peterson was *my* Gavin Peterson.

"Gavin! Oh, my goodness! Congratulations!" Without thought, I was in his arms, hugging him, and he was rubbing my back. Home. He always felt like home. When I pulled away, his eyes were focused on my chest. My robe had fallen open, and I quickly pulled it closed.

Gavin spread his arms across the back of the couch and shrugged, "Not like I haven't seen it before, Nova."

"Yeah, but you shouldn't be seeing it now."

"You're not involved with anyone, are you? I mean, I follow you on social media. No talks of a special someone, and if you are, it isn't serious, because you checked in here alone." Gavin smirked. I would kill Shelly when I got back.

A knock at the door saved me from having to respond to him. I got up and let room service in. The young girl's eyes bugged out when she saw Gavin sitting on the couch. I thanked her, tipped, and sent her on her way.

Gavin was next to me in an instant. Too close. His cologne filling my space, suffocating me. He ran a finger down the back of my neck. He knew that touching my neck turned me on, and I did not resist the contact. I should have, but I didn't. He had me pressed against the table — I couldn't move even if I wanted to. I didn't know what I wanted at that moment. Gavin was my Achilles heel, and resistance was futile.

I had never fucked two guys within hours of one another, but I was about to break that. I think.

Bitch, what you talkin' about, you think? I shook my thoughts from my head and pushed him back with my ass. He took that as an invitation, grabbed my hips, and began to kiss and lick the back of my neck.

I didn't want to, but I moaned out loud and whispered his name.

Gavin sighed into my skin. "God, I missed you, Nova."

"I...I..." Rendered speechless by his touch, I melted into him.

Gavin was safety and danger wrapped up in one hard body. My robe was pooled on the floor around my bare feet, and he continued licking a path down my spine. He licked his way down to the crack of my ass--leaving a cool trail behind. With a strong hand, he bent me over the table as I pushed my food away to lay flat against the cold marble. The contact sent a shiver through my body as his tongue played with my hole.

"Gavin."

"You like that, baby?"

"Oh, God, yes."

"Open up wide for me."

I took my hands and pulled my cheeks apart so he could get a better view of all my glory. His tongue eased its way down to my pussy, and I felt no remorse that someone else had journeyed there hours before. It felt too good and familiar to be worried or cared about.

"Let me see you."

I turned around, and he was sitting shirtless on his knees, tasting me on his lips. His body was better than I remembered years before.

"God, you're beautiful." Gavin ran his hand up my calf, and when his palm met my knee, he lifted his leg over my shoulder and sucked on my clit.

I could feel myself throbbing against his tongue, holding on so that this moment wouldn't end, but when he slid one finger in and pressed against my favorite spot, I came undone. My knees buckled, and I felt as if I was going to fall at any moment. Gavin was there, holding me up. Still tasting my nectar as if it was the last thing he would taste forever.

Gently, he placed my foot back onto the floor, and he stood. He stared into my eyes, willing me to believe everything he ever told me; I fought back with my own gaze. Trying to get him to see all the hurt and pain he caused.

"Fuck, Nova." He grabbed my face and kissed me. The kiss was rough and tender all at the same time. He poured so much emotion into that kiss as I resisted giving in to him. He would just be another fuck. Nothing more. Nothing less.

"That is what I plan on doing to you, Gavin." I took a step forward, forcing him backwards. As we moved slowly, our tongues danced into one another's mouth. He sucked on mine as I undid his belt buckle, unsnapped the button on his jeans, and pulled away to get off his pants. Greeted by his hard dick, I licked his shaft, then moaned around the head of his dick. His was the first I had ever seen, the first I ever touched, the first I ever fucked. It was me who pursued him when I was fifteen. I had asked him to teach me how. I loved him, and he loved me. It was the right thing to do. We fumbled around at first, laughing away the nerves, but we figured it out. All these years later, we still seemed to just figure it all out.

Gavin's legs hit the couch, and I nudged him into a seated position. I gave him pleasure with my mouth as he tried to fight his orgasm. He loved it sloppy and wet, so I gave him that. Spit. Hands. Sucking. Licking. Just little teeth. I knew him better than he knew himself when it came to his dick. I worshiped Gavin in the only way I knew he would appreciate, but he couldn't take it anymore and made me straddle him.

"Gavin." I tried to protest the fact that he hadn't put a condom on. I was clean, but I had no idea what he had been up to all these years.

"I'm clean," he answered without me asking out loud. "I promise. Trust me."

He felt so good as I rode him. I took it slow at first, my head thrown back, my mouth wide open in silent ecstasy.

He growled and said, "Fuck this." He flipped us over, never leaving my folds. Gavin fucked me long, hard, and perfectly until I was screaming his name and calling out a God in heaven that I had no idea if he existed. If he did, then this was the bliss I have been searching for all of my life.

When I came, it was hard while his fingers danced across my clit. My juices flowed between us, and he watched as he made it happen.

His eyes found mine asking permission. He always asked before he came. I nodded, and he slammed into me. One. Two. Three. Four. Five. His warmth filling me to the brim; pumping until his body quaked above me.

Once we caught our breath, reality set in. I did not freak out the way I did with Chaz. I just laid there, his body next to mine, gently brushing my hair out of my face.

Gavin smiled. "Hungry?"

"Yeah, but my wings are cold." I got up and went to the bathroom. I could hear him ordering more room service, and then the cork on the bottle that sat chilling on the table popped. Moments later, when I had the shower running, he walked in with two glasses. I took one and sipped from it. It was just what I needed. We stepped into the shower together and washed off.

Once dry and out of the shower, our food had arrived, so we sat laughing about our childhood.

"That was my nerd stage! You can't hold that against me." Gavin laughed.

"Yeah, okay, Gavin. You loved anime. More than me, I used to think." I sighed at the memory.

"Nah, never." Gavin got this weird look on his face, and I knew he was about to say something serious.

Before he could, I sat up straight and faked a yawn. "It's late. I have to be at my parent's house early."

I had seen that look on Gavin's face plenty of times when he got shot down by a girl he had a crush on. Part of me felt bad, but the other part knew he needed to leave before we went down a path of no return.

"Yeah, you're right." He began gathering his things. "I will see you tomorrow. Three, right?"

"Yeah. Three." I followed him to the door.

He turned to me. "Nova, I —"

I put up a hand in protest. "Don't."

He pulled my hand to his lips and kissed them. Once again, I was fighting the urge to ask him for more. I didn't have to ask because when he dropped my hand, he grabbed my waist and stepped in for a kiss. He kissed me, and I did what I said I wouldn't. I asked him to stay. There wasn't any more sex, but there was plenty of kissing and cuddling until we both fell into a peaceful sleep.

4

CHAZ

My alarm screamed at me at 7:15. I rolled over, did my morning hygiene routine, and headed to the gym in my basement. I ran five miles before I stopped to answer my phone.

"Yeah?" I was breathing heavily into the phone.

"Did I interrupt something?" Monique's voice purred on the other end of the line, and my dick jumped. I had met her through a friend a few months back, and she was reliable for when I needed to get my dick wet.

Right now, I was too stressed to think about sex. I could very well be the reason why someone could lose all that they had built; just for some fucking accounts that I probably could get on my own. That was the problem with society, today, always wanting the easy way out and not trying to just duke it out with fate.

"Hey, Mo. What can I do for you?" I wanted her off my phone so I could lift a bit, then ignore the paperwork I should be getting to while we were closed for the holiday weekend.

"God, Chaz, could you be any shorter with me?"

Her feelings were the last thing on my mind. "Yeah. Actually, I could be."

She sighed. "Well, I need you today."

"I'm unavailable."

"Please. Just a few hours. I have a thing at my aunt's house, and I really don't want to go alone." She paused, "I will pay you in blowjobs."

Monique could fuck, but she was terrible at giving head. I stifled a laugh. "I'm good. Will there be food?"

"Yes! My aunt gets busy in the kitchen. She's actually my great aunt, but she cooks like a big mama." Monique was always giving too much information and rambling on. "Pick me up at like 2:30 p.m., and drive one of your nice cars." The call ended before I could answer. I guess I was getting a home cooked meal after all.

It was Christmas morning, and the only living relative I had lived across the country. My younger sister Charity owned a yoga studio or some sort of wellness center in Southern California. I invested in her company a few years back, and I haven't seen her since she asked for the loan. She was living her best life with her girlfriend, Mel, and their two dogs. She didn't have time for me, and I rarely had time for her. It was okay. We worked that way. However, we were there for one another when we needed to be.

I really wished that I hadn't answered the phone because no matter how good that meal sounded, I wanted to just stay at home. My refrigerator was full, all the best channels were waiting for me to flip mindlessly through them, and my balls ached to be released as many times as they — or my hand — could handle. I hadn't had a day off with anything to do in a long time. Sure, I could get some of that paperwork done, but that was not my priority for the weekend.

In the shower, I pictured Nova down on her knees sucking me off. I don't think I ever had a better set of lips do the job. It was like she was in love with my dick, and I didn't have one complaint. I just wished she was here and not in my imagination. Her number was saved in my contacts, all I had to do was call, but I wasn't sure when all the shit was going to hit the fan, so I probably should get to her before it did. The palm of my hand met the skin of my hardness and wrapped around it with a tight grip. My imagination got the best of me and as I thought of Nova's juices pouring all over me, I came. Much too quickly. What the fuck was wrong with me?

Frustrated with the hundreds of channels I was paying for with nothing to watch, I decided to actually get some work done. In the three hours that I worked, I managed to clear out my pending file, and I was feeling proud of myself. By the time I made a quick sandwich and got dressed, it was time to go pick up Monique.

When the car eased in front of her apartment building, she came sauntering out in this tight red dress that didn't reach what anyone would think was appropriate to wear to their great aunt's home. She had to be freezing. Shit, I had the heat blasting and still shivered when I saw her get in.

Monique had this silly look on her face when she slid onto the leather seat of my car. As I eased onto the normally busy street, she was giggling like she had a secret. Regret started to settle in because I was beginning to think she was high on something.

Looking over at her, I finally spoke up, "You okay?"

"Yeah." She paused and her smile grew wider, "I was wondering if we could try something."

"Something like what?"

"Road BJ." She looked as if she had come up with the greatest idea anyone had ever come up with it.

I'm not going to lie, Monique was looking fine as hell in that dress. She was probably cold, but she still got my dick hard. My answer to her was pulling out the proof, and she actually clapped with glee. Annoying as she was, I needed to get Nova and that situation out of my mind. Too bad Monique was terrible at giving head. I mean, she got the job done, but her skills weren't as well-groomed as Nova's.

She damn near got the front of my pants wet from all of the spit she thought I enjoyed. Too many teeth. Couldn't deep throat for shit. This shit was whack. However, I came in her mouth, and she had the nerve to gesture for me to pull over so she could spit.

Her mood went from giddy to pissed by the time we pulled up to her aunt's house. As I stepped out of the car, I noticed that the house was a nice little cottage on the more decent side of this neighborhood. Opening the trunk to my car, I silently fist pumped myself for having a spare pair of slacks. I slid in the back seat to change and Monique was still in the passenger seat, huffing and puffing.

I rolled my eyes. Part of me wanted to just ignore her; if she was mad and I was having a terrible time, this would be an easy way out for me. However, the other part of me did not want to deal with Monique's spoiled ass attitude. "Everything okay, Mo Money?" She liked it when I called her that stupid shit. I had said it one night when she talked about her hair salon and how good it was doing.

I watched as her attitude fizzled a bit. "No."

Well, we are playing the one-word answer thing, I guess. Staying in the back seat, I leaned forward, deepened my voice, and whispered, "Is Sir going to have to bend you over his knee for a proper answer?"

More fizzle. "No. I just —"

I placed the palm of my hand on the back of her neck and gently squeezed. She loved this shit, too much. To the point where it was not enjoyable for me, so I told her we would only play on special occasions — which turned to never.

"No, what?" My mouth was close to her ear, my tongue darted out on instinct, and I traced a line from the top to the lobe.

"No, Sir." She whimpered.

"Now, tell me what's wrong."

"Sir, I just don't like it when you cum in my mouth."

"Is that so?"

"Yes, Sir."

"I apologize. I got caught up in the moment."

"It's okay."

I sighed. "It isn't okay. Not if you don't like it. It won't happen again." Literally. I decided right then and there that she was going to get cut off. "Let's go inside and get some of this bomb ass food you keep talking about."

Once inside, it seemed like Santa and his elves threw up in this house. Then, Rudolph and his crew came in and took a shit on the carpet. To say that the owners overdid it with the decor was putting it lightly. Like, who buys these things? Upon further looking, a lot of the decoration looked homemade. Most of it looked as if it was done at the hand of a child. I flipped one ornament over, and it had the initials "NW" written in tiny print at the bottom.

A gruff voice rang out behind me, "It is a little over the top, but she saved every single piece of our girl's artwork and displays it with pride."

I turned around to a tall man standing with a smile on his face. He had a full head of grey hair and a nice round belly. I probably had him by at least four inches, but he held himself up as if he was seven feet tall. There was something familiar about the man, but I shook the feeling away.

I reached my hand out to him. "Chaz Jones."

"Albert Wilcox, but call me Al. So, you're Monique's flavor of the week?" I didn't quite hear the question because I was too focused on his name and the familiarities. It couldn't be.

Monique came around the corner with a woman with hips for days and an apron on. She was short and had grey hair to match her age. Monique told me she was in her seventies, but I didn't believe her. Al's smile grew wider once he noticed her come in the room. I wanted a lady on my arm that I could smile at like that. I could feel his love for the woman without even looking at him and when she saw him, she returned the sentiment. I wanted a love like that.

"Mama, did you want me to take the ham out of..." I could pick out her voice in a room full of people as it trailed off probably because I was standing in the middle of her mother's living room.

"No, the oven is on warm." She looked at her daughter. "Girl, what is wrong with you? You look like you saw a ghost."

A white boy walked up next to her and placed a hand on her shoulder. "You okay, babe?"

Him calling Nova a "Babe" sparked a bit of jealousy in my brain as I watched her to make the first move.

Before she could say anything, a few cell phones chimed in the room, and Monique added to the noise by screeching. "Oh my God. Nova, I think you should look at your phone."

Well, there goes the shit. Hitting the fan.

PART II
THE BLACKMAIL

5

SHELLY

I LIVED A DECENT LIFE. My condo was beautiful. My sex life was healthy. Really healthy. I had a few guys I could call on to meet every need that I had. One who loved to give head. One that could fuck well. Another that ate ass, but was a good kisser. I could never find just one person that could do all of the above all at once. I made do with what I had.

Something was missing, though, and I knew just what it was. My own empire. I wanted what Nova had. She just sat back receiving the credit — and the money — while we did all her work. Realizing this, I put my plan into action. It took me about seven months of planning before I could talk her into getting out of my hair so I could see everything come to fruition.

Don't get me wrong, Nova was a fair boss, but when you wanted to be your own boss and had no way of doing so, it was a hard pill to swallow. I tried to convince her to let me take on her newest client as my own. I saw full potential in the woman, and I'm guessing that Nova did too when she shot me down. Prior to Ava DeLece acing her audition to be the leading lady in Denzel's next film, I tried everything to sabotage her business. Nova was quick to act on all cases, recovering quickly, and that fueled my fire even more.

I was skimming off the top. Her accountant Joe, better known as my ass licker, helped me to be able to purchase my condo. I still needed more. I desired more, and I would stop at nothing to get it.

While out to have drinks with a few coworkers, someone mentioned the possibility of setting up Nova and ruining her credibility. That is where I got the idea. No one likes a woman on top, and they especially didn't like a slutty one. I received a few names from clients of men who had things set up that was along the lines of pay for play. One lived near Nova's hometown. We had been talking for a while, and we finally agreed that when Nova's clients fell into my lap, he would provide his service to them every time, if they were in a town where he had his drivers.

I tried to convince Nova to visit home for weeks, but she would brush me off and say that she had too much work to do. Finally, the holidays rolled around, and I took matters in my own hands to speak with Mrs. Nadine. After a two-hour conversation, I managed to get her to call Nova and tell her that she needed to get home for a visit. My plan was in motion because she was on a flight back to her hometown.

Joe was sitting on the floor sucking on my pinky toe, he slid a hand up my leg as I sent a text to Chaz complaining about my boss complaining about him. Oh, yes, Joe sucked on any body part I put in his mouth, and I loved it.

Me: She's a bitch, so make sure you fuck her good.
Chaz: She's not all that bad. You sure this will work?
Me: Yeah. Getting cold feet?
Chaz: Nah. But I will fuck her just right.
Me: I don't know why you won't fuck me.
Chaz: I don't mix business with pleasure.
Me: UGH! Whatever, she just said that you can't drive for shit.
Chaz: So, it's working.
Me: Come on, let me get some of that dick.
Chaz: I'm good.
Me: But I'm not. I've heard stories.
Chaz: So have I.

Me: What is that supposed to mean?
Chaz: I'm good.
Me: Fuck you, Chaz.
Chaz: I'm about to fuck your boss. But you can pay me, Shelly.

I threw my phone down on the couch.

"Everything okay, honey?" Joe said in between moving from my pinky toe to my big toe.

"Don't start that 'honey' shit, Joe. I'm not in the mood." I kicked my foot so he would stop.

"Come on, I have something that will put you in a better mood." Then he grabbed his crotch, squeezing it.

"Please, I can't do anything with that teeny weeny in your pants."

I got up to go wash off my feet, Joe was hot on my heels. "You don't have to be such a bitch, Shelly."

Turning to look at him, he stopped dead in his tracks — realizing the mistake he made. Joe was balding and needed to let go of the hair that circled his head from one ear to the other. He had a beer belly, but claimed to not drink beer, and he looked like his balls stank. He was short, stubby, and when I looked at him, I imagined his dick being this weird shade of pink to match his light-skinned complexion. The only thing going for him was his money and the ability to help me set up Nova. He was nice, but I wasn't trying to fuck.

"What did you call me?" The top of my head burned from anger.

Joe squared his shoulders and grew a pair. "A bitch."

"Have you lost your —"

Joe cut me off, "No, I think you lost your fucking mind. You sit up here acting all fucking high and mighty like I can't take you down with a snap of a finger. I know it all."

"Really, Joe? You've been scheming for years!"

"But that won't come back to me. Everything will lead right back to you with a push of a button. Go ahead and try me." Joe stood there while I calculated my next move.

"I thought we were in this together?" I tried to sweeten up my voice and run my hand down his arm gently.

He swatted me away from him. "Please, Shelly, we all know that you are out for just yourself." Joe pushed past me towards the living room to collect his belongings.

"You're leaving?"

Without looking at me, he answered, "Don't act like you care now. Don't worry, I won't do anything to mess up your little plan."

As I made my way towards Joe, I slipped my nightie down my body. "Don't go."

I could see him debate on whether or not he would stay. He sighed. "Shelly, you have made it very clear that all I am good for is using my mouth on you."

"I just don't like fucking more than one man at the same time. That is messy."

"Funny how you're trying to set up Nova for the same shit you do."

This was going to be harder than I thought — I needed him in a good mood, or he will find a way to pull out of everything. I needed that money in my account each week until everything settled in my favor. Getting down on my knees in front of him, I conjured up my best puppy dog face and begged, "Please?"

Zipping down his pants, I held my breath and waited for the stench to hit my senses. When the smell wasn't anything unnatural, I sighed with relief and pulled his dick out.

"Well, well, well. What do we have here?" Joe was packing! I could work with this.

"You taking that back now?" He smiled down at me.

I shrugged my shoulders. "I figured you could use a hug, but with my mouth."

Joe laughed, but sucked in a breath of air when I put him in my mouth. "Damn, girl. I usually don't like for women to go down on me because they can't usually take me in all the way, but you're fitting this whole dick down your throat," he moaned.

I pulled him from my mouth. "You like that, honey?"

"Oh yeah, shit, but I want to fuck. Let me fuck that tight pussy. Lick your ass and put it in there too."

"My dude, you're not putting this thing anywhere near my ass.

Nope." I put him back in my mouth and prayed that he would forget about fucking me. Mister Good Fuck was on his way over in an hour, and I did not need Joe stretching me out before our session. I did a few tricks with my tongue and the back of my throat, and he was cumming in a matter of minutes. I even swallowed just to show how special he was.

"Damn, Shelly, I wanted to fuck." He grabbed his dick and tried to get it hard again.

"Next time, honey." Getting off the floor, I made my way to the sink for a glass of water. "I have some things to finish up to get ready to send to the press. I appreciate all of your help. Enjoy your holiday with the wife and kids tomorrow."

I know, I ain't shit, but I get what I need out of people.

Joe went in to kiss me, and I snapped my head back. "Seriously, Shelly? We haven't moved to another level."

"Go home, Joe."

With that, he grabbed his shit and left.

After cooking a quick meal for myself, eating and taking a shower, my phone pinged. Chaz had come through, and I was about to get my piece of the pie.

6

NOVA

GAVIN WOKE me up with his head between my legs, and after I called out his name about twenty times, we got dressed and had breakfast downstairs. Apparently, I missed a lot in his life because he was very well known and had to let his staff know that he wasn't to be bothered while he was there. Our conversation flowed like we never stopped talking. I was so confused about us — I don't know if the bricks were being put up or torn down. Right now, I was just going with the flow.

Gavin and I arrived at my parents' house at about ten this morning. My mother eyed me weirdly when we arrived, and I knew I had some explaining to do later. My father seemed oblivious like it was normal to waltz in with the boy that caused his daughter those tears all those years ago. They both welcomed him in like the son they had told him he was to them back when we were snotty-nosed kids that played video games all night long together. Being home on Christmas was just what I needed. My mother was right.

Later into the afternoon, Gavin found me standing at the front window watching the snowfall. I missed this white shit. We got the occasional snow, but not like upstate New York. I had countless white Christmases growing up, and it was like the universe was sending me a silent reminder as to how special this all was. Home. Family. Christmas. Snow. It was magic watching it fall, but a bitch to drive in.

Gavin whispered in my ear, "It's beautiful, but not as beautiful as you." He slid a long box in onto the windowsill. "Merry Christmas, beautiful."

"Gavin, I didn't get you anything. I'm sorry." I picked up the box. "I can't accept this."

"You can, and you will. I had a promise to keep to a fifteen-year-old girl who stole my heart." He pushed the box towards me. "Mama Nadine made me wrap it. It was in a nice bag before, and she said that her daughter deserved wrapped gifts." He chuckled, and I could hear my mother berating him over his gift and ignoring the fact that he got me a gift in the first place.

I opened the package carefully, inside was a beautiful tennis bracelet from Tiffany's. I had been eyeing this very one for the last few months, so I knew how much it cost, and I could never accept this. "Gavin, I —"

Gavin pulled the box out of my hand, removed the bracelet, and placed it on my wrist. It was beautiful. X's with the O's as a diamond. "I promised my first love that I would buy her one when I was able to do so."

"Not quite this fancy."

He smiled. "You're worth it."

I leaned in and kissed him. I poured my thanks into the connection of our lips. When I pulled back, Gavin had that look in his eyes, and I reached down to confirm my suspicions. He was hard as a rock. Not saying a word, we walked up the stairs to my childhood bedroom.

"I've always wanted to fuck you here." He laid back on my purple comforter and watched me as I undressed.

"You got to like a second base in here." I pulled my sweater over my head.

Gavin sighed. "Yeah, bring me back to those days."

"Why go back when you can finally fuck me in here?"

He jumped up, and we fell back onto the bed. "You were always the smart one out of us."

Us, ouch. That included Abby, my ex-best friend. My heart mourned for her, the baby and our lost friendship on one side, and on the other, anger pumped through the veins.

Gavin noticed the change in the air and quickly tried to bring us back by kissing me.

"Did it hurt?" I rolled to my side and asked him.

He pushed some of the curls out of my eyes then laid back with his hands behind his head. I got a nice view of his abs. "Yeah. I've always wanted to be a dad. So, yeah. It still stings a bit."

Happiness flowed through me when he was honest and open. I did try to talk to him when it happened. Both of them pushed me out and away. It was okay. But it wasn't. So, him speaking about it now, gave me great relief that we could possibly grow. It didn't have to be in an intimate way, I just wanted my best friend back.

Playing with the skin at the top of his jeans, I felt a shiver run through his body. "Are we doing this? Here?" "What are you afraid of?" I smiled at him as I crawled down his body.

"Turn around." Gavin was watching me unbutton his pants with hooded eyes. I gave him a questioning look and his smile deepened. "I want to suck on that pretty little clit while you suck on my big dick."

"Oh, you want to get freaky, freaky?"

That brought out a full-on laugh from his lips. "That's freaky to you, babe? Well, you ain't seen nothing yet." He sat up, reached for my hips, and flipped me on my back. I was laying between his legs with mine up in the air.

"I doubt I will be able to get you in my mouth from this position."

He shrugged his shoulders. "I'm a patient man."

My pants were off and on the floor before I could respond. His mouth on me before I could inhale my next breath. He took my clit in his mouth, sucked, then blew on it. My body was shaking as I tried to stifle my screams. I pulled a pillow over my face to help muffle the sounds, but it was quickly removed from my face and thrown; joining my clothing.

"I want to see you come undone." Gavin slid to his knees to get a better angle and lowered my legs to the bed.

"What happened to doing one another at the same time?" I managed to get out as his tongue darted in and out of me. He was tasting me, the joy in his eyes made me crumble as an orgasm ripped through my body. When I was at the peak of the orgasm, Gavin inserted a finger or two into me — I couldn't really tell where because I was busy screaming his name — and began fucking me with them.

"Shhh...babe, your parents are going to hear you."

I moaned my answer back to him.

"Damn, you look so good down there." He was hovering over me, watching as the wave washed over me and subsided. "Fuck it." Gavin was pushing his hardness into me causing me to scream out louder. It was too late to try and hide it now. Call this payback for all those years my parents subjected me to the same exact thing.

Gavin came quickly, quicker than he had ever done before. He turned red, and I grabbed his face between my hands. "Aw, babe, don't feel bad. It happens to everyone."

"Shut up, Nova. You know this shit doesn't happen to me, but the thrill of being in here and how tight you are, I just couldn't help it. You feel so good. This feels so good."

I jumped up. "Do you want the bathroom first, or should I go?"

"Nova."

I sighed. "I will go first."

Practically running into the bathroom, I shut the door and leaned against it. The tennis bracelet was shining on my wrist, laughing at me, taunting me. Wanting a shower, but settling for warm wipe down, I was ready to get Gavin out of here. The chances of that were slim to none. Clothes back on and hair fixed in the mirror, I exited the bathroom.

He was sitting on the bed with his head in his hands, looking up to talk when I walked into the room. "Nova..."

I didn't let him finish what he was going to say, I just walked right out the room and into the lion's den. I could smell the ham baking in the oven and thought that it had been in there entirely for too long. Maybe my mother was losing her cooking magic.

"Mama, did you want me to take the ham out of..." I couldn't get the rest of my question out of my mouth because I thought the den was going to consist of stares and questions about the noises coming from my room — butt because of a six-foot-four bag of chocolate standing in the living room talking to my parents, whom I happened to have met and fucked in the backseat of his car yesterday.

"No, the oven is on warm." My mother looked at me, and I instantly knew she could tell something was up. "Girl, what is wrong with you? You look like you saw a ghost."

Gavin chose that moment to walk in and place a hand on my shoulder. "You okay, babe?"

I internally cringed at the endearment and opened my mouth to speak, but was cut off by my cousin Monique shrieking in her annoying voice, "Oh, my God. Nova, I think you should look at your phone."

My phone was going off like crazy during the session with Gavin, but everyone knew I was on vacation, so it could wait. I pulled my phone out of my back pocket to find ten voicemails, twenty missed calls, thirty text messages, and twice as many emails.

I clicked on the first email from a blog site that I often worked closely with; the owner and I had a good rapport. The subject line read: *IS THIS TRUE?!?!*

As I read through the email, I felt as if the floor had been pulled from underneath me, and my breakfast was about to empty onto that non-existent floor. When I read the words, **"I'm trying to hold off on posting this, but the powers that be are trying to get a jump on the story. Please respond. Video attached."**

There were voices around me, but I couldn't process what was being said. I clicked on the attachment, and there I was in all of my glory, nude and sucking dick. Unfortunately, the email was sent over two hours ago. It was too late for my team to get ahead of this because they all were probably finding out at the same time as I was.

I looked up at Chaz who was looking at me with a hint of awareness and a lot of concern. "Did you do this?"

He didn't respond, but Gavin jumped right in with a slew of Nova questions. "You know him, Nova? What did he do? Do you want to sit down? Are you okay, Nova?"

I stepped closer to Chaz. "Did you do this?"

My mother's phone rang, thankfully Monique had some sense in her to tell her not to answer the call. Monique looked from me to Chaz and back to me again. "What can I do?"

That snapped me into action. "I need you to run to my hotel and grab my laptop. I will make some calls." She moved into action immediately. Monique was my very first assistant. She had her flaws, but when it came down to it, she helped me get my business off the ground running.

Chaz stood in the middle of the floor staring at me. Gavin had his phone in his hand and must have been brought up to speed when I heard him say, "What the fuck?" under his breath.

Monique walked back into the room and shouted, "Chaz, I need a fucking ride!" He hesitated but moved to leave out of the house.

"Nova Lee Wilcox, what on earth is going on?" My mother was fanning herself like she was out of breath. "Joyce from the women's club just called saying that she knew I was up to no good raising a child at such an old age."

My father turned to her. "She what?"

I rolled my eyes. "Mama, tell Miss Joyce to mind her fucking business for once."

At the same time, both of my parents shouted, "Nova!"

Needing to regroup and figure out what I was going to do, I went up the stairs to my bedroom. Gavin had straightened up the bed once I left him alone, but I decided to sit on the floor next to it. Opening up the file on my phone, I watched it about ten more times. I scrolled through all of the blogs calling me every name in the book. Twitter was even worst. Before I knew it, I had gone down the rabbit hole and couldn't climb back out.

When I read the tweet that said, "Who is this man, and can I have one?" I was done. Why is he protected, and I'm shamed? It doesn't make any fucking sense.

I dialed Shelly, and she answered right away, "Oh, my goodness, everyone is calling trying to get a statement."

"I'm sure they are. Look, I need you to move my flight up to tomorrow morning."

Shelly sighed in the phone. "That's going to be next to impossible."

I was fed up at this point. "Try!" I ended the call.

My next phone call was to my lawyer. "Miss Wilcox, I've been trying to reach you."

"I know, I actually was enjoying my vacation." Managing to conjure up a bit of a chuckle. "Leon, what do I do?"

"Look, I've seen this happen to a lot of celebrities."

"I'm no celebrity, I just represent them."

Leon sighed, too much of that was going on around me, I should have been the one sighing and crying, yet, here I was holding it all together. "We can sue for slander."

"Is that really your best legal advice?" I wanted to hang up. "No suing. Should I release a statement?"

"I was attempting to make you laugh. Relax. I'm emailing you a few options that we drew up. They are in order of the best to worst. Call me back after you have gone over them." He paused for a moment, "Nova, you will be fine."

My phone beeped, and it was Shelly calling me back. "It's Shelly, I gotta go."

"Nova, before you go, I just want you to know that word on the street is that someone close to you leaked the video."

Just like that, the dam broke. There had been some underhanded playing on my team, and we could never track who it was. Shelly, my accountant, Joe, and I spent many nights trying to figure out who was trying to steal accounts from me. Clients would tell me to watch my back because someone was contacting them to try to get them to leave and join them. The only reason why they knew it was from my team is because they were contacting them in ways that only I had access to. That was for the protection of myself and my clients. However, we couldn't catch the person.

This was the ultimate betrayal, and the tears were no longer able to stay locked in their ducts. I just sat there with tears pouring down my face. Justin Timberlake watched me with a smile on his face. Christina Aguillera danced to the tune of my heartbreak. While Cleo from *Set It Off* snarled at me — she was ashamed, sending me vibes to get up, and set it off just like she did. I let a few more tears fall before I called Shelly back.

"I tried to get you a flight out, but the earliest I could do is Tuesday morning." Shelly was short with me, and it made me stop and think. It couldn't be Shelly. No, Shelly applied shortly after Monique told me I was getting too big for her to handle and that I should bring someone else on. That was a year into my business; Shelly was loyal to a fault. She would never do anything to hurt me.

"Tuesday? That is one day earlier than what I was supposed to leave out." I pinched the bridge of my nose. "I will call the pilot myself."

"Wait! Let me try again."

"Shelly? What the fuck is going on?" The door to my room flew open, Monique entered with my laptop bag.

"I just figured you would want to be around your family, during this time."

I wanted to fix my mouth and curse her out, but my blood pressure was high enough. "No, I need to get back as soon as possible. I said tomorrow. As in December 26th. If you can't get the job done, let me know."

"I will get it fixed." She huffed into the phone. I hung up.

Monique was looking at me warily. "Chaz and I had a nice conversation. He was your driver yesterday?"

I shook my head. "Not right now, Mo."

"I could pick that dick out of a line-up, I knew it." Monique sucked her teeth, crossed her arms, and watched me.

Standing up, I mimicked her stance. "Is there a problem?

Monique, I don't keep track of who it is you're fucking, and if I knew he been up in you, I would have never looked twice at him."

"Really, Nova? You say that like I'm nasty or something."

I wanted to tell her that fuck yeah, she was. Remind her about that little gangbang or train or whatever the fuck she wanted to call it with a few players from the football team. However, I was currently being slut-shamed, and what one does behind closed doors, or in my case, backseats, was their business.

"Monique, I'm not saying anything, but you're standing here accusing me of dick stealing when that is not the case." I took the bag from her and watched her tentatively. "Not the case one bit. So, either help me or get out."

"I'm trying to help."

"Doesn't seem like it, but a glass of wine would be great."

Monique laughed. "I'm not your little bitch anymore."

I paused, "Mo, can I ask you something and expect you to be perfectly honest?"

"I don't know how to be anything else."

I rolled my eyes. "When you worked for me, did you ever feel like I used you, or that you would want to get even with me?"

Monique sat on my bed. "No." Then she voiced her thoughts aloud. "I mean, you had your moments when you were stressed. I felt like you may have barked at me a little louder and harder than usual, but you paid everyone well, and outside of those stressful moments, you were a great boss."

I sat next to her and put my head on her shoulder. "I think one of my employees is trying to sabotage me."

Monique, the hood chic that she always will be, started going off. "Who I gotta fuck up, 'cuz?"

"Lord, Mo, sit your crazy ass down. We are professionals now, we handle things differently."

She leaned up against my desk. "You have to be pressed up or really jealous of someone to try and ruin everything someone built. Do you have any ideas who it is?"

"Nope. My lawyer just confirmed my suspicions, but I have no idea who would do this to me." I looked up at her. "Did you ask Chaz about it? Is he still here?"

"When I asked him, he told me that I should mind my business. I thought it was strange, but I was just like whatever, and he left as soon as he dropped me back off, which is probably for the best because Gavin was standing on the porch pacing back and forth. What's up with that? And did he give you that bracelet because, damn, Nova!" I had my suspicions about Monique doing drugs a while back. She had gotten into some financial issues with her salon. I paid her well and let her stay with me to save for her dream spot, so when she called me needing bail money and a couple g's to pay someone back, I took one look at her and knew she was up to no good. Today, she looked put together, but she must have taken something before she came back here. I didn't say anything, though, today was not the day.

I pulled up a few sites and some photos of me entering my hotel room; Gavin arriving and us leaving together had leaked. More fuel to the fire.

7
SHELLY

Nova was getting on my last fucking nerve. I wanted all of this controversy to make her hide under a rock, but she wanted to fight back. Of course, she would fight back. I should have seen this coming, but when I told Joe what was going on, he said he had a friend that owed him a favor. That is when I received surveillance footage of her high school sweetheart arriving at her hotel room. Surely this would stop her from wanting to fight this through.

Joe was on his way over with a plate from his house. When I told him that I was going to order some Chinese, he yelled at his wife to make a big plate and that he was bringing it to his boy. I hope she could cook because I was really looking forward to my broccoli in brown sauce and the hunger was real.

My phone rang. "I'm still trying to reach the pilot, I told him to enjoy his holiday. He must have set his phone down or something. I'm so sorry this is happening to you."

Nova took a deep breath. "I called him myself."

"Oh."

"Yeah."

Not too sure if I was supposed to respond to that, I said nothing.

"Did you think that I wouldn't?" Nova was pissed.

"Nova, I'm sorry, I just think that you shouldn't rush back home."

"It isn't your job to think, it is your job to do as I ask."

"Wow." I don't know why I was offended.

"Look, I'm sorry. Some pictures leaked and things have gotten worse. Leon is about to release a statement on my behalf, and I just want to get home." I could hear her typing something on the other end. "I'm sending over my flight itinerary for Sunday. He's booked until then, thanks to you for not catching him earlier like I asked!."

At that point, I was done with this conversation. Joe was walking in with a damn Christmas sweater on and my plate of food, so I couldn't care less what she had going on. By this time Monday morning, I would be taking over her accounts. I had already sent a few anonymous DMs to her clients asking if this is the type of representation they wanted to be under and to contact me if they desired better. One person sent over their information. It was only a matter of time.

"I really am sorry. I won't ever do that again." I faked concern.

Nova hung up without responding — it was at that point that I began to actually worry that she knew it was me. I had to get ahold of Chaz to make sure he was holding up his end of the bargain.

"Hello?" Chaz's voice was super sexy.

"Hi, Chaz."

Joe stopped what he was doing in my kitchen. "You are not on the phone with another dude while I'm here."

Rolling my eyes at Joe and his insecurities, I wanted to remind him that he had a wife at home. I refrained because I needed him now more than ever.

"Shelly?" Chaz interrupted my thoughts.

"Sorry, Chaz. Hey. Everything good on your end?"

"I told you that I would call if something went wrong. Were those pictures you took?"

I smiled. "I do what I have to do to get what I want."

"You could have just worked for it like the rest of us." Chaz sounded like he was regretting what he had done.

"Do I have to worry about you, Chaz?"

"Nah. I'm good." He hung up.

I was over people hanging up on me. I was over being pushed to the side and treated like pond scum. I desired what Nova had. At an opening night gala, dressed in the best gown, she smiled and flaunted in front of the cameras while I stood to the side holding her bag and grabbing drinks all night. I had received my own invitation but was treated as hired help. Invisible all night, I decided that I wouldn't take it anymore.

Looking at Joe, I also decided at that moment that I no longer wanted to be number two. "Joe?"

He was making his way over with my warmed-up plate which was smelling delicious. Handing me the plate, he flopped down next to me and kissed my cheek. "Yeah?"

"I want you to leave your wife."

Joe looked at me and smiled. He took my face in his hands, leaned in, and kissed me. I let him, and it felt good. It felt like someone finally wanted me. The plate ended up on the table, and he ended up on top of me. With his dick inside of me, I thrashed, moaned, and scratched at his back. Feeling full with something that I couldn't quite put my finger on, I came with his name on his lips. Sweat beaded on his forehead as he flipped me over and fucked me from behind. I came again, and he followed soon after.

Out of breath and spent, Joe sat me up and said, "Shelly, I won't be coming over anymore."

"What?"

"Everything is done with us. Your last check will be deposited next week. I'm out." He wiped his brow, got up, and began dressing.

"You're not fucking serious, are you?" I grabbed his arm, and he yanked it away.

"Have you seen my wife? Why would I leave her for you?"

I had seen his wife. She was beautiful, but he always complained about her, so I just assumed that he was unhappy. "Get out!"

"My pleasure. I hope all of this," he gestured to the home his checks helped me build —"brings you happiness. Remember, if you get caught and my name comes up, you won't make it to the jail cell

H*e for the Holiday

that you will rot in for years." With a wink and a smile, Joe walked out of the front door.

With every fiber of my being, I tried to fight the tears that kept on coming. I wasn't sad. I was mad that, once again, I was pushed aside like I was nothing.

8

NOVA

I sat on the floor in my old bedroom and poured over every detail, every blog post, every tweet until Gavin came in and told me that my mother demanded me to eat or else.

Everyone was quiet when I made it to the dinner table. Night had fallen, and I had to be honest, I was hungry after all the work I had just done. Leon submitted my statement, and it seemed that it was working. I went with the third one he sent; it was perfect. Of course, I gave my friend the jump on it because she at least had the decency to give me a heads up and ask if it was true before running the story.

NOVA WILCOX, HOW DARE YOU?

Nova Wilcox releases a statement that asks the media, "How dare you?" In the short, but to the point disclosure, Nova makes sure she makes us all feel ashamed, including myself. She writes: "How dare you? In a time where 'Me too' is a movement with woman empowerment, I ask you all, how dare you? What I do in my personal time is none of your business, and you all should be ashamed for slut-shaming a woman that knows what she wants.
I am unaware of the person or persons responsible for leaking these intimate moments, but I am aware of those that shared it, joked about it, and slandered my name. So, once again, how dare you?"
Nova, as a fellow woman of color and as someone trying to succeed in this hard world, I apologize for playing my part in all of this. I had no right for the sake of a story.

I wasn't expecting her to end her blog that way, and it made me feel good. Leon didn't think it was smart to go with that one because it came off with an angry black woman. However, I *was* angry, and I am a black woman. Now I had to get to the bottom of who did this and why.

Everyone watched me as I silently ate my food, and I wanted to scream at them all for it, but I knew they couldn't help being

53

concerned. Placing my fork down, I looked up at everyone. "What the hell are y'all staring at?"

Monique was the first to burst into laughter. "You, bitch! We're trying to figure out if you're okay or not! Damn."

"Well, ask that then! I'm trying to enjoy my mama's cooking." I dug back into my plate.

Gavin sat across the table from me, he kicked my shoe to get my attention. When I looked up at him, all he did was wink. Fucking winking got me in this situation, but of course, I melted right there on my seat and was wet in an instance.

My phone buzzed.

Gavin: Meet me in your room in twenty minutes.

Me: I have work to do.

Gavin: Work can wait.

Me: This all has me so stressed, I just want it to be over.

Gavin: Let me relax you before you get to it.

Me: Gavin. I don't have time.

Gavin: There is always time for sex.

Me: True, but I have to find out who did this!

Gavin: I'm sure they will be here tomorrow.

Attached to that last text was a picture of his dick, and I opened it just as my father leaned over to talk to me, "Who you talkin' to? Put that damn thing down and enjoy your family. Work can wait." The fact that Gavin had just said that and I almost got caught looking at his dick, I barked out a laugh. Gavin shook his head, and my family looked at me like I was crazy.

Gavin: You can't hold water.

Me: I didn't say anything.

Gavin: All obvious that you and I were up to no good.

Me: Correction — you are up to no good. I'm just minding my business eating.

Gavin: Nova, I really need to talk to you.

I put my phone down and avoided eye contact with Gavin for the rest of my meal. I don't know why he always wanted to get serious and talk. My parents called it a night shortly after I gathered my things and kicked myself for not renting a car because I was stuck riding back to the hotel with Gavin.

He let out a long breath. "I feel that you think I am trying to like confess my love for you, but I'm not." I'm sure my face made him rethink what he just said. "No! I mean, God, you know I love you. Shit. What I'm trying to say is that I'm not trying to get down on one knee. I was just trying to fucking apologize to you, Nova. No more bullshit excuses about being drunk. I did what I did, and I am so sorry for ruining us. For hurting you. I'm sorry. I do love you, and I want you to know that I am always here."

I grabbed his hand and squeezed it. "I appreciate that so much, Gavin. Sorry I was avoiding this conversation. I seriously thought you were about to propose or something stupid."

"Shit, I was that night. That's why I was so fucking drunk. I was nervous."

I turned to him in his seat. "What?"

"Yeah, I went to tell Abby, show her the ring, and next thing I knew, I was waking up to the two of you in a screaming match." His voice was soft and quiet.

"Gavin, we were so young."

"I didn't care."

"Why are you telling me this now?" I watched the trees fly by through the window.

"I thought you should know that I didn't choose her. I will always choose you."

Gavin's car slid smoothly into the valet at the hotel, and there was a gaggle of people standing outside. As soon as I stepped out, lights flicked, and questions flew. I was pulled back into the car, and my door was slammed shut by an attendee outside. Gavin flew out of the parking lot quicker than I could process what was going on.

Once I focused on the world around me again, Gavin was speaking to someone on the phone. "Yes, gather her things and have them sent to my place."

When he ended his call, I crossed my arms and asked, "What makes you think I want to go back to your place?"

"You want to deal with that back at the hotel? Fine."

"Shit, I'm sorry. It's okay. Merry fucking Christmas to me." I was sulking. I was sure that statement would get everyone to leave me alone.

"Don't do that." He pulled out his phone. "I'm guessing yours is dead."

He was right. I scrolled through a few blogs titled: *"HOW DARE US?" "WILCOX COMES OUT SWINGING!" "WE ARE SORRY — NOVA THE COMEBACK QUEEN."* I smiled to myself and sighed with relief.

Gavin's car pulled up to a beautiful house surrounded by a huge gate. Punching in some numbers on the keypad, we sailed through and parked at the rear of the home.

"You live here?" I asked stupidly.

He laughed. "Yeah, Nova, I live here." We entered, and the house was decorated in greens and reds for Christmas. "Aunt Jean went a little overboard."

I sucked my teeth. "Please, no one goes as overboard as Nadine Wilcox."

"Very true." Gavin took my jacket and hung it on a hook.

"So, your aunt lives with you?" I asked as he showed me around.

"Nah, she just visits and redecorates when she feels the need to. This time around, the need led to holiday cheer."

"I like it." I smiled as we rounded a corner that led to a row of bedrooms.

Gavin pointed to the end of the hall. "That is mine. You can basically play pick a room, any room, and go for it."

"You live here all alone? This is way too much space."

Gavin shrugged his shoulders. "I was hoping to fill it someday, but the one for me got away." I sighed, hoping he wouldn't take it any further than that. Thankfully, he didn't. He kissed me on the cheek and whispered, "Merry Christmas, Nova Lee Wilcox. If you want to shower, I will leave a pair of sweats and a t-shirt for you. Let me know if you need anything, make yourself at home."

I opened the first door and immediately looked for an outlet to plug in my phone. Once I did, I left it there to get a little charge before going to work again. A shower sounded nice. The bathroom was immaculate. When I saw the tub, I opted for a bath instead. I must have dozed off because I woke to cool water and Gavin sitting on the edge of the tub rubbing my face with his thumb.

"Tired?" he asked.

"Warn out." I took the towel he offered me.

"I came to tell you that Boom just arrived with your things, but found you asleep in here." Gavin got up, and I took all of him in as I dried off. God, he was sexy. Shirtless. Grey sweatpants. Lord, the things I wanted to do with that dick print, but I waved the thought out of my head. Sex got me into trouble, maybe I need to lay low.

"Who is Boom? And why did his mama name him that?" I followed him out of the bathroom and back to the bedroom.

"Head of my security."

"The fuck you need security for, you own a hotel?"

Gavin's head tilted back as he laughed. "Not for me, my hotel. I do need security at my hotel, Nova."

"Oh. I'm just so out of it."

He walked over and kissed my forehead. "Okay, get some rest. See you in the morning."

When he left out, I decided that I wanted to sleep naked. The bed and comforter looked too comfy to ruin that with clothing. The coolness of the bedding wrapped around me and this was the best mattress I had ever laid on.

Once my phone was turned on, I sent Gavin a text.

Me: This is the most comfortable bed I have been in.
Gavin: Enjoy.
Me: Thank you.
Gavin: You're welcome.

I decided that work could wait until the morning and that sleep was more important. Something in Gavin had changed. I tossed and turned for about twenty minutes before I decided that I needed to go find out what it was. I threw on my black nightie and padded down the hall barefoot to his room. I didn't bother knocking, I just barged right in. It was dark in his room, but I could hear him breathing softly from the bed sitting on the far wall. His room was huge and smelled like him. Way too much room for one person.

I slid in the bed with him and nudged him. Gavin blinked his eyes. "Nova?"

"What's going on with you, Gavin?"

"Nova." He pushed his wet hair out of his face, turned on the bedside table, and put his glasses on. I forgot that he wore glasses. "Nova, you have been running from me all day, you don't want to hear what is going on with me!"

"Oh." When he said that, my suspicions were affirmed. Gavin was on a mission to get me back and for good.

So, I decided to give him the next best thing. I slid on top of him and kissed him deeply. Rubbing my wetness against his bare leg, the friction almost made me cum. He was only in his boxers, and it felt good to have his body heat against me. At first, he hesitated, but after a while, he let me lead.

"I owe you. And I think you owe me."

Throwing the cover back, I turned around and placed my pussy right over his face. As I worked his boxers down, Gavin took little bites at my thighs. I found a comfortable position and lowered myself onto his face greedily, and he obliged. Slithering my tongue up his shaft, I felt him moan between my folds. God, this felt so good. I took his head in my mouth and sucked up the precum. He tasted like he had a few drinks before bed, but I didn't mind. I was going to enjoy this. Trying not to focus on his tongue dancing on my clit, I took him all the way down until my nose touched his balls. I stuck my tongue out and let it slide up his veiny hardness as I pulled him out of me.

Gavin sighed against my thigh and kissed it. "Shit, Nova. You learned some tricks over the years."

"Mmhm," I agreed with him deep in my mouth.

"Oh, no, I'm not going to last with you doing that."

I made the sound again and squeezed the bottom of his shaft. This allowed him to catch his breath a bit. Turning around, I pulled my nightie off and slid down onto him. This was the perfect fit. One thrust and he was hitting my favorite spot. Gavin lifted me and topped me from the bottom. He fucked me hard and good while I tried to withstand the pleasure. I unraveled several times, oozing down his dick until he came hard mixing with my juices.

Gavin went into the bathroom and came back with a warm rag. Cleaning me, he touched me in ways that had me shaking with another orgasm. I didn't think I could take anymore.

The next morning, I woke with a new pep in my step and set out on a mission. Gavin had to leave early to get some work done at the hotel and left me with the keys to his Jeep. After some research and receiving the paperwork I requested from Leon, I set out to get the final piece of the puzzle.

1
CHAZ

PACING THE FLOOR, I had a sleepless night after dropping Monique off at her aunt's house. The look on Nova's face when she saw the leaked video shattered me, and I prayed to go back in time to erase it all. More information had leaked, and one headline on a blog read, ***MORE SCANDAL FOR NOVA WILCOX, WILL THIS RUIN HER CAREER?*** There were photos of the hotel owner, Gavin Peterson, walking into her room not even hours after I dropped her off, of them leaving the next morning and sharing breakfast, together.

My stomach clenched. I don't know if it was the fact that this Gavin character got to share all this time with Nova or that the media was eating all of this up. I honestly didn't think that Shelly would move so fast with the information. I assumed she would wait until the holidays passed so everyone could enjoy them, but you know what they say about assumptions.

The doorbell rang, and I went to answer it. Surprised at the person standing at the door, I stepped aside and closed it behind her.

"I just want to know who it was that put you up to all of this and what they promised you." She sat down on a chair at the table and pulled out some paperwork.

"I have no idea what you're talking about." I watched her for a moment. "How did you find out where I lived, Nova?"

"You would be surprised the things you can find out on the internet, Chaz." Nova was all business. "What did they promise you?"

I sighed. "Business."

"For someone whose limousine business revenues about one point seven million dollars a year, it doesn't seem like you needed the cash."

"I wanted to expand. They promised me that."

Nova scoffed. "You did pretty well in the few years you were in business, don't tell me you couldn't do that on your own."

Sitting next to her, I had to figure out how to get her to see my side of things. "Nova, I really didn't think all of that through. It was quick, easy money. I was tired of working so hard."

"So, you decided that media slut-shaming was the way to get you what you wanted?" Nova shuffled the papers, found the one she wanted, and slid it to me.

"What is this?"

"It's a contract."

"For?"

"Guaranteeing you every single client that I have on the books." Nova slid another paper over.

"And this is?"

"Paperwork that my lawyer will submit to sue you and take everything you've got." Nova sat back in the chair and raised an eyebrow.

She was fucking sexy as hell.

I copied her movement. "What does either have to do with the other?"

"Giving me your contact will save your business. If not, well..." She trailed off, but I could finish that sentence for her. I wanted to bend her over my dining room table and fuck her.

Shaking the thought from my head, I looked at the papers in front of me. Shelly didn't even offer me anything in writing. How would I know if she could hold up the end of her deal? Nova must have gotten ahead of this whole scandal to be here and was ready to take down whoever was trying to take her down.

Do I betray Shelly? I had nothing to lose. If I don't give Nova the information, I have everything to lose.

"Who's this Gavin dude?" I went out on a limb to get more from her. I don't know what it is about her, but I was drawn to something.

I could tell my question threw her off a bit. "What does that have to do with anything, Chaz?"

"Inquiring minds would like to know."

"You're not at liberty to know." Nova watched me for a moment. "What do you decide?"

"The obvious choice."

"That is very wise. I just need a name."

I looked up at Nova and fought the desire to ask her on a date after all this was said and done. She wanted a name, so I gave it to her. "Shelly."

EPILOGUE

NOVA

I'M NOT GOING to lie, it hurt when Chaz said her name. I confronted her, and she squealed like a pig. I wanted to be all about second chances for her, but I just couldn't bring myself to forgive her for all she had done. Joe and I poured over my finances, and it also appeared that she found a way to steal from me too. To say I was shocked was putting it lightly. No charges were pressed, no public humiliation, I just sent her on her way and wished her luck in the future.

Believe me, which was a hard pill to swallow — just letting someone walk out the door without any repercussions. I was hoping the universe would send me good karma in my life for doing the girl a solid by not sending her to jail. My fingers are still crossed.

Gavin and I are still a thing, if you can call it that. When he's in town, we meet up and the same when I'm home. I go home a lot more often now to see my parents. I noticed that they were getting up there in age, and I needed to slow down and spend some time with them.

Business is great. It is better than great. After all of the drama, I had some A-listers that wanted to be represented by a company with a leader like me. It felt good. Chaz and I have our business arrangement, and he was able to expand across the East Coast. He is currently in the works of opening up an office in California. It felt good to be able to turn a negative into a positive. We would have lunch or dinner with one another from time to time. He tried often to get in my pants, but a girl doesn't kiss and tell.

ABOUT THE AUTHOR

T. Ashley lives in Connecticut with her three crazy children, their father, and their cat. She received her bachelor's degree from Belmont University in Nashville, TN where she discovered her love for playwriting. You can catch her on stage at local theatres where she gets to express herself in other creative ways. She really does not know what else to say because, yeah...

Made in the USA
Columbia, SC
21 July 2020